SKYSCRAPERS

SKYSCRAPERS

HOW AMERICA GREW UP

BY JOHN B. SEVERANCE

HOLIDAY HOUSE / NEW YORK

Library of Congress Cataloging-in-Publication Data

Severance, John B.
    Skyscrapers: how America grew up / John B. Severance
        p.   cm.
    Includes bibliographical references and index.
    Summary: Details some of the innovations that enabled the
building of taller and taller buildings, describes the various
schools of skyscraper architecture, and explores the history
of several famous skyscrapers.
    ISBN 0-8234-1492-2
1. Skyscrapers—United States—Juvenile literature.
[1. Skyscrapers.] I. Title.

NA6232 .S44 2000
720'.483'0973—dc21
                                             99-051842

For Sylvia

CONTENTS

The Great Pyramid of Cheops is high enough to be called a skyscraper, but the term is commonly applied only to tall buildings of the nineteenth and twentieth centuries.

CHAPTER ONE

INNOVATIONS

"There is no economic need to build skyscrapers anywhere," Philip Johnson once said. Coming from Johnson, an architect who participated in designing many of the best-known skyscrapers of the twentieth century, the comment is startling. It provokes thought about the various purposes of tall structures and calls for a clear idea of what makes a building a skyscraper.

If remarkable height alone defines a skyscraper, some of the first ones were built more than four thousand years ago by the ancient Egyptians. The original 482 feet of the Great Pyramid of Cheops had enough height for a fifty-story building. But in forty-six centuries of sitting in the desert, it has not had a significant effect on how people live. It is a tomb, a monument of death.

Later, around 280 B.C.E., Egyptians built a tall building for the preservation of life. It was an immense lighthouse whose beacon warned sailors of the danger of wrecking their ships on Pharos, a peninsula at the entrance to the Mediterranean harbor of Alexandria.

Archeologists think the structure was about 450 feet tall, but they cannot be sure because in the fourteenth century the Pharos lighthouse was toppled into the sea by an earthquake. Nevertheless, along with Cheops, it was among the Seven Wonders of the Ancient World.

Throughout history, religious fervor has often inspired the creation of huge buildings. Some examples are the Mayan pyramids in Mexico, Hindu temples in India, or the great cathedrals of medieval Europe. Neither these buildings nor the massive buildings of ancient Egypt have been called skyscrapers, but they do have one thing in common with the nineteenth- and twentieth-century tall buildings we know as skyscrapers. It is the power of the human ego. Johnson explained it as a desire, fueled by personal power, to reach for a "dominant height." An enormous tomb, a huge lighthouse, colossal houses of worship, and modern office towers all require the ambitious drive of kings, high priests, popes, or business executives. These are the personalities needed to inspire and supervise huge construction projects.

Modern skyscrapers differ from previous tall structures because of their use of technical innovations. Many architectural historians say that the first skyscraper was the first building to include a steel skeleton in its support system. Other historians, however, have pointed out that steel alone could not have made taller and taller buildings possible. A number of other innovations were also essential to skyscrapers. These include wonders now taken for granted, such as elevators, telephones, electric lighting, and modern plumbing.

For example, most people will not happily climb more than five flights of stairs. So before passenger elevators were invented, office buildings were rarely more than four or five stories high. Although freight elevators were used in English warehouses as early as 1835, they were not considered safe for human passengers. It was not until the invention of a safety brake, which prevented elevators from crashing to the basement when a rope broke, that passenger elevators could be installed.

Having reached an office on the ninth floor, however, who would

Cologne Cathedral in Germany, the largest Gothic church in northern Europe, is an example of massive religious architecture inspired by the human spirit.

want to go all the way back to ground level to use the bathroom? In the mid-nineteenth century plumbing technology developed rapidly. Many of the fixtures, traps, and fittings still used today were invented then, including systems for creating good water pressure on higher floors.

In the twentieth century other new materials and techniques made it possible to construct skyscrapers far taller than any nineteenth-century buildings. The architects and engineers of those early skyscrapers probably never imagined diesel earthmovers, colossal cranes, air-conditioning, fusion welding, thermal glass, computers, or even plastic pipes. Modern technology enabled the construction of the groves of tall buildings now standing in cities throughout the world.

The Petronas Towers in Kuala Lumpur, Malaysia, represent the recent appearance of super-skyscrapers in the Far East. The skeletons of these twin towers are made of cast-in-place concrete.

Some of these buildings, including a few designed by Philip Johnson, are famous. Many more are so ordinary that even the people who work in them could not say who designed them. Real estate agents are fond of saying that the three most important things in their business are location, location, and location. If many people want to live in the city and many companies want to have offices in the city, there is a demand for skyscrapers.

There really is no "first" skyscraper. The debate over what building qualifies as the first could go on endlessly because it depends on what features are selected to define that word. The significant story is how, in the past one hundred and fifty years, a number of innovations in construction engineering came together. In this blink of time, there has been a growing need for living quarters and workplaces to be stacked up in locations where there is a limited amount of space. We have named these stacks skyscrapers, and they have changed forever the way people live and work.

Elisha Graves Otis demonstrates his elevator safety brake in 1854.

CHAPTER TWO

GOING UP

In 1854, during the second season of a world's fair called the New York Crystal Palace Exhibition, an inventor named Elisha Otis presented an astonishing demonstration to a fascinated crowd. Otis struck a dramatic pose on a platform that had been hauled high in the air while his assistant, brandishing a large knife, hacked at the thick rope that suspended the platform above the gaping spectators. Some people turned away in horror, but when the cable parted, the platform did not plummet to the ground. Instead, it only bumped a little, and remained where it had been hoisted, held in place by safety brakes that Otis had invented two years earlier.

Otis was born in 1811 in Halifax, Vermont. Always a tinkerer, he earned his living in his younger days working in a bedstead factory. By 1852 he had established a freight elevator factory in Yonkers, just a bit north of New York City. In 1853 he demonstrated a steam-powered elevator during the first season of the Crystal Palace Exhibition. Up to that time most freight elevators were operated by human beings pulling ropes.

The Crystal Palace Exhibition in New York City (1853–1854)

These two innovations, the steam elevator and safety brakes, could hardly have had a more appropriate location for launching than the New York Crystal Palace. The vast building that housed the great fair was itself an innovation inspired by a similar building constructed in London for the Great Exhibition of 1851. Designed by Sir Joseph Paxton, the British building was a framework of iron supporting walls and roofing made of large panes of glass. The technology, much copied in Europe and America, demonstrated the capabilities of two materials that would revolutionize the construction industry. For a person of Otis's inventive and entrepreneurial nature, it was not only a good time to be at the fair, it was also a great time to be in New York.

In the nineteenth century the vigorously expanding commercial district of the city was concentrated in the lower end of the island of Manhattan. Banks, law firms, and insurance companies clustered along the waterfront around the southern tip of the island. The nearly land-locked harbor that sheltered the bustling shipping industry was safer from storms than any other seaport on America's Atlantic coast. In addition, this port had access to inland trade through the Hudson River valley and the Mohawk River valley. In 1825 the Erie Canal connected Buffalo, New York, on Lake Erie through New York State to Albany on the Hudson River, making it possible to ship goods by water from the Great Lakes to New York City and then on to Europe. Because businesses on its crowded waterfront were growing rapidly, New York was running out of commercial space near ground level, and office buildings had to grow upward.

New York City in 1883. The New Jersey shore is visible at left, and the Brooklyn Bridge at right.

The taller they grew, the more they needed elevators. If, however, a lift cable were to break, the fall to the bottom of the shaft would also be greater, resulting in at least some broken bones and perhaps a few deaths. The device that Elisha Otis demonstrated at the Exhibition was a pair of bars attached to a large leaf spring on top of the elevator. The tension on the rope hauling the elevator caused the spring to pull the bars inward, away from the walls of the elevator shaft. If the rope broke, the spring was released, forcing the iron bars against a vertical line of notches in the shaft walls, thus stopping the elevator's fall. In 1857 Otis built the first elevator equipped with these new safety brakes, making it suitable to carry passengers. After the Civil War his business flourished and the elevator company continued into the twentieth century.

The first building in New York to be equipped with passenger elevators was the eight-story Equitable Assurance Society Building, completed in 1870. The exterior masonry structure and facade were designed by the firm of Gilman and Kendall. George B. Post, who had studied engineering at New York University, was in charge of the interior engineering, including elevators and the iron framework. He designed the shafts and supervised the installation of the elevators that, perhaps because Otis had died in 1861, were not built at the well-known Otis factory, but at another factory in Boston. Originally the Gilman and Kendall plans did not call for elevators, but Equitable's founder, Henry Baldwin Hyde, insisted on them. Post, too, believed in them so strongly that he made a guarantee to other Equitable officials who were in doubt and offered to be "personally responsible for renting the upper floors if there was any difficulty in doing so."

Perhaps more significant than his faith in elevators was Post's expertise in another nineteenth-century innovation, iron support skeletons. For centuries, large buildings had been made by placing brick upon brick or stone upon stone Strength and stability were added by placing layers of mortar or cement between the stones. Floors and roofs had to be supported by timbers, but the major upward thrust of buildings was

The Equitable Assurance Society Building designed by George B. Post

supported by masonry. In terms of support Egyptian pyramids are not much different from the medieval cathedrals built more than three thousand years later. Metal had been used for supplemental reinforcement by the Romans, but it was not until the late eighteenth century that iron began to be used as the main support for a few buildings in England and France. In the early nineteenth century, it became common in commercial structures in England and then in America.

It is important to understand the difference between cast iron and wrought iron. Cast iron is made by pouring molten iron into a mold. When cooled, the carbon content of the iron causes it to become brittle. Cast iron beams laid horizontally are not the best support for a broad factory floor. They can snap like dry sticks if overloaded with heavy machinery, such as printing presses, especially in a fire when extreme temperatures cause cast iron to weaken. Wrought iron, on the other hand, is shaped by hammering the heated metal or rolling it under extreme pressure. It contains almost no carbon, and when used as floor beams, it can support a great deal of weight, even in a fire. In mid-nineteenth-century buildings cast iron was often used as upright posts to reinforce and sometimes decorate masonry walls. Wrought iron was generally used for horizontal support in floors and roofs.

The development of wrought iron technology had another important use in the engineering of tall buildings. Cast iron pipes were adequate for draining wastewater out of a building, but first the water had to be pumped to the upper floors. In 1848 a company in Philadelphia began to manufacture high-quality wrought iron pipes, fittings, and valves to deliver pressurized water to the many floors of multistory buildings. The sophisticated plumbing was needed to service bathrooms and also to heat buildings with either steam or hot water. As New York became the financial nerve center of a growing nation, the United States became the leader in the technologies of cast iron and wrought iron.

At the same time the Equitable Building was going up, the eight-story Broadway Central Hotel, designed by Henry Englebert, was built at Broadway and Bond Street. At 149 feet, it was 7 feet taller than the Equitable. It had iron floor beams, plumbing throughout, and mirror-walled elevators. In its best years the Broadway Central was the grandest hotel in the city, attracting glittering actresses, foppish playboys,

The elegant Broadway Central Hotel, designed by Henry Englebert, was seven feet taller than the Equitable Assurance Society Building.

and wealthy business tycoons. In the mid-twentieth century it became a seedy residential hotel, and in 1973 the facade collapsed onto the sidewalk. Nevertheless, some architectural historians have ranked the Broadway Central among the first skyscrapers.

Two years after the completion of the Equitable Building, George B. Post won the design competition of the Western Union Telegraph Company for a building to be built at the corner of Broadway and Dey Street in lower Manhattan. As well as three elevators, the structure had

Completed in 1875, the Western Union Building was, for a time, the tallest building in New York.

other remarkable features. "The entire twenty-three-foot-high eighth floor, where the telegraph operators worked," writes one historian, "was unobstructed by walls or columns except for the four iron pillars supporting the iron clock tower." In addition, if the municipal water pressure failed during a fire, the building had its own backup pumping system. The ten-story skyscraper no longer exists, but when it was completed in 1875 it was the tallest building in New York.

Throughout the next three decades, Post designed many complex buildings, including several huge private mansions, two state capitols, and the New York Stock Exchange. His forte, however, was tall buildings, which is why he was described by the prominent Chicago architect Daniel Burnham as "the father of the tall building in New York." But Post's reputation need not be limited to New York. He designed many skyscrapers in cities such as Buffalo, Cleveland, Montreal, and Pittsburgh. It is sad that in the twentieth century many of his buildings were demolished to make way for taller skyscrapers. If the Equitable Building and the Western Union Building were still standing, they would illustrate the brilliance of George B. Post as an architectural pioneer.

George B. Post, engineer and designer of many early tall buildings

*The Great Chicago Fire, October 9, 1871, as seen from
the west side of the city*

CHAPTER THREE

THE PHOENIX

Fire has always been a serious danger in crowded cities. Ancient Rome had a disastrous one in 64 C.E., and in 1666 London had a terrible conflagration that burned for five days and destroyed nearly all of the city. After every bad urban fire in history, cities have established new building codes outlining specifications for fire escapes and fireproof building materials. But new generations often have to learn the lessons of history all over again.

The chance to make lots of money can easily distract people from the lessons of past disasters. This was true of Chicago during the middle years of the nineteenth century, when its population grew from a few hundred to half a million. Hordes of people were attracted by the booming city whose location on the shore of Lake Michigan was a bustling crossroads of commerce. The Michigan and Illinois Canal linked the Great Lakes to the Mississippi River basin so that goods could travel entirely by water all the way to New Orleans. A network of railroads connected various regions of the eastern, southern, and western sections of the American continent through the hub of Chicago.

Amid this exuberant urban growth, buildings made with lumber shipped from northern forests were hastily slapped up, using the innovative balloon-frame method. This type of construction was much cheaper and faster than the centuries-old post-and-beam method that required muscular laborers to move huge timbers and skilled carpenters to shape joints and pegs. No one knows who invented balloon framing, but it was first seen in Chicago. The new system created wall support with two-by-four-inch-thick beams called studs set upright about a foot apart on a horizontal floor beam called a sill. The studs were capped with a horizontal two-by-four called a plate, and the whole framework was held together with another innovation, cheap factory-made nails. The method was jokingly called "balloon" because, under construction, the delicate-looking cage-type frame made it seem as though the finished building would blow away like a balloon on the breeze. In fact, the popular technique was at least as strong as the post-and-beam method, and today the majority of houses built in the United States are balloon-framed.

As wooden buildings sprouted like mushrooms on the prairie, wood was also used for floors and roofs in the few buildings, mostly banks, that had masonry walls. Many of the muddy streets were paved with blocks of tarred pine, and the sidewalks were boards laid on frames built a few feet above the damp ground. Private houses had barns or sheds in back for hay to feed the horses. Cows were also kept in some of these buildings, along with firewood and kindling to heat cooking stoves.

The popular story, repeated in newspapers across the country, was that a cow owned by Mrs. O'Leary of 137 De Koven Street kicked a lit kerosene lantern into some hay and started the Great Chicago Fire. The fire did, in fact, begin at the O'Leary place in the southern end of the city. At an inquiry after the fire, however, it was learned that early on the night of October 8, Mr. and Mrs. O'Leary and their children were already in bed, and the cows were safely in their stalls. All lights were out. A neighbor across the street saw a tongue of flame lick out of the barn behind the O'Leary cottage and aroused the O'Learys. They managed to douse the flames that scorched the back of their house, but the fire ignited the board fence that surrounded the lot and then jumped to the neighbors' cottages.

The flames were fanned by the southwest wind that was gusting off the prairies, and soon several blocks were on fire. Aided by the prairie wind, the intense heat of the fire created powerful updrafts that carried sparks and small chunks of burning debris into the sky. Wherever these landed, new fires sprang up, and by midnight the inferno had jumped the south branch of the Chicago River. Half-dressed people and others in only their nightshirts rushed through the firelit streets, clutching bundles of possessions or rescued toddlers. During the early morning hours, the towering wall of flames swept northward through the center of the city, chasing thousands of fugitives before it. One reporter

Panic-stricken citizens carrying the aged, sick, and helpless and endeavoring to save the family treasures from the Great Chicago Fire

The Great Chicago Fire as seen from Lake Michigan

claimed that it was moving as fast as a man could run. The streets were crowded with ragged and soot-covered citizens, making rich and poor look the same. Fleeing from the furnacelike heat and billowing smoke, thousands waded into the Chicago River and the chilly waters of Lake Michigan, many holding small children above the waves.

Around midnight on the night of October 9, as the flames were consuming a doctor's house on the north side, a light rain began to fall. Presently it intensified. "I never felt so grateful in my life as to hear the rain pour down at three o'clock this morning," a north side resident wrote to her mother. "That stopped the fire." Three days later the *Chicago Tribune* published an upbeat editorial. "Though four hundred million dollars worth of property has been destroyed, Chicago still exists," it trumpeted. "Let the Watchword henceforth be: *Chicago Shall Rise Again.*" In little more than a week, temporary housing was knocked together for nearly all of the thousands of families who had been made homeless, and sheds for small businesses sprang up among the ruins. As the acres of charred debris were cleared, gifts of food, clothing, and building supplies began to arrive by rail from other major cities.

At about the same time that George B. Post's career was getting started in New York, a construction boom began in Chicago. It was halted briefly by the financial crash that swept the country in 1873, but even that could not prevent greedy contractors and dishonest city officials from ignoring Chicago's new fire safety code. In 1874 another serious fire temporarily slowed the industry. Eventually the message got through to builders and politicians alike, especially when insurance companies began refusing to insure buildings that did not conform to the fire safety code.

The mood of the city was like a carnival attracting people from all over the country hoping to make their fortunes. Many did get rich and a few made millions. The wealthier businessmen built extravagant homes with their profits. Glittering theatres and elegant hotels sprang up to accommodate other businessmen visiting from out of town. In 1882 the first mechanical cable car, an improvement on horse-drawn trolleys, took its first official trip in downtown Chicago. Loaded with city politicians and other dignitaries, it started out in front of Marshall Field's department store and amazed thousands of spectators by trundling twenty blocks in half an hour. The last cable cars are still a transportation curiosity in San Francisco, but the first ones in Chicago soon circled the downtown district that came to be known as "the Loop." Beyond the Loop, however, it was not cable cars that defined Chicago. It was the railroads.

Miles and miles of rails were constantly being added to the numerous trunk lines entering the booming town from all points of the compass except the east on the lakefront. The prairies surrounding Chicago on all sides but the lakefront might have provided ample room for the young city to spread out. The arteries feeding the expansion of commerce, however, also served to constrict it. In the haste of construction, the railroad beds were laid flat on the ground through congested areas. Railroad companies did not care to spend the extra time and money to build elevated tracks above the busy streets or dig tunnels under them. As a result, slow freight trains many blocks long sometimes held up city traffic for hours. Like New York surrounded by water, Chicago surrounded by railroad tracks was becoming a prisoner of its own prosperity.

As commercial activity increased, businesses drove land prices higher with their feverish search for additional office space in the center of town, the only area where there were no railroad tracks. Escalating prices within a limited district created a squeeze that made a two-dimensional concept of real estate useless. Although it lay on the horizontal prairie, the city would have to become vertical. Chicago had to grow up.

In the same year that the cable car made its debut in the Loop, a tall building was completed on the corner of Monroe and Dearborn Streets. It was called the Montauk Block and was designed by the architectural firm of Burnham and Root, which had made a name for itself designing private mansions for wealthy businessmen.

One biographer reports that in high school Daniel Burnham "excelled in both athletic and artistic projects, but, as with many potential artists, not in scholarship." His family wanted him to go to Harvard or Yale, but he couldn't get into either college, so he took a job as an apprentice draftsman with the firm of Loring and Jenney. In this office "with William L. Jenney, the great architectural pioneer, he had his first . . . training in architecture." Working in the same office were several other future architects, including Louis H. Sullivan, who would become one of America's greatest. Then, like many restless young men of the time, Burnham headed West, hoping to make a fortune mining silver in the new state of Nevada. He failed.

Returning to architectural work in Chicago, Burnham met a fellow draftsman named John Root. Born in Georgia, Root studied engineering at New York University, worked for a year with James Renwick, designer of St. Patrick's Cathedral, and then for J. B. Snook, designer of Grand Central Terminal. Attracted by the architectural opportunities created by the Great Fire, Root went to Chicago where he and Daniel

*Daniel Burnham
of Chicago*

Burnham eventually became partners. Burnham supplied the business drive and Root the aesthetic genius.

The same sort of partnership was seen in the firm of Adler and Sullivan, another successful Chicago group. Like William Jenney, Dankmar Adler was an engineer who had gained most of his knowledge in the Union Army during the Civil War. His outgoing nature, plus his practical business sense, made a fine balance with Louis H. Sullivan's design skills and artistic instincts. These capabilities had been refined at the Massachusetts Institute of Technology (MIT) and the Ecole des Beaux-Arts (School of Fine Arts) in Paris. Today Sullivan is well known for his belief that the decorative outer wall or facade of a building should echo its inner structure. In his own time this philosophy was often at odds with other trends, but it influenced his students, the most famous of whom was Frank Lloyd Wright. Eventually Adler and Sullivan parted company, and Sullivan tried to go it alone in New York. He designed a number of significant buildings around the country, but he never again achieved the prominence he had enjoyed in the Chicago partnership.

Burnham and Root's Montauk Block

Partnerships, however, were becoming essential to the planning and design of the urban landscape. The complexity of modern architectural firms was foreshadowed in the teamwork of firms like Adler and Sullivan or Burnham and Root.

Burnham and Root's Montauk Block was an investment project of two brothers in Boston, businessmen Peter and Shepherd Brooks. Peter Brooks was very sharp about detail and expense. For the facade and other outside walls, Brooks insisted that there be no projections to catch dirt, and he was equally picky about the interior. "The less plumbing, the less trouble," wrote Brooks to his architects. "It might also be advisable to put in wire for future electric lights." Later, when some new designs had been submitted, Brooks wrote back, "Colored glass is mere nonsense, a passing fashion, inappropriate in a mercantile building and worse . . . it obstructs the light. Strike it all out."

Brooks must have been pleased with at least part of the building's foundation, because it was cheaper than the older method developed to support buildings on the deep layer of soggy sand and clay beneath Chicago. Previously the basement of a masonry building concealed a number of huge, square "feet" in the form of pyramids of stone and concrete. Root calculated that on one side of the Montauk, where the plans called for fireproof vaults on every office floor, the colossal weight would require pyramids squeezed side by side in the basement. This would leave no room for service equipment such as pipes, ducts, and a furnace to heat the building during the bitter Chicago winters. To solve the problem, Root invented a "floating foundation" with layers of Portland cement and crisscrossed steel rails to make a two-foot-thick pad capable of supporting the vertical columns of a massive building. For many years Chicago builders used Root's innovation, until new techniques were developed for sinking pilings down through the swampy soil to the bedrock that lay a hundred feet below the city.

When it was finished, the ten-story Montauk Block was a Chicago landmark, and one historian writes that it was "probably the first building ever to be called a skyscraper."

*Under construction: Administration Building of the
World's Columbian Exposition, Chicago 1892*

CHAPTER FOUR

MRS. JENNEY'S BIRDCAGE

One evening in 1883 Elizabeth Jenney was reading a large and heavy book, perhaps an encyclopedia or maybe the family Bible. Her husband, the Major, came home tired and brooding about a construction problem, and as she stood to greet him, she set the volume on a birdcage next to her chair. Mrs. Jenney's birdcage could not have been the round domed structure sometimes seen in cartoons about birds and cats. Most likely, it resembled the antiques that occasionally turn up in flea markets and yard sales. Imagine a flattopped, wire-walled structure with internal supports dividing the space into a few tiny rooms in which birds can hop around.

The Major stared at what his wife had just done. If such a delicate structure could support that heavy weight, he thought, perhaps a steel cage could be the skeleton of a large building. No version of the story relates the reaction of the birds inside the cage or even if there were any, and there is no record of Mrs. Jenney's feelings about her husband's abruptly diverted attention. The tale does, however, illustrate a thing or

William Le Baron Jenney, engineer who first used steel beams in constructing a tall building

two about William Le Baron Jenney. First of all, since the story was probably invented by the Major himself, with a good deal of help from his friend and main building contractor, Henry Ericsson, it shows that Jenney was a man of some imagination. More importantly, it illustrates the marvelous simplicity of his architectural innovation.

Born and raised in Fairhaven, Massachusetts, Jenney sailed around South America to San Francisco during the California gold rush of 1848 and then on to the Philippines. When he returned to Massachusetts, he entered the Lawrence Scientific School at Harvard but became bored and in 1853 went on to the Ecole Central des Arts et Manufactures, a well-known engineering school in Paris. After graduating with honors, he worked in Mexico but soon returned to Paris where he studied drawing with James McNeill Whistler, a fellow American who later became a famous artist in London. Jenney then went to work for a railroad investment firm and returned to the United States in 1861 to meet the company's president, William Tecumseh Sherman, who, anticipating war, urged him to join the army. During the Civil War Jenney served on the staff of General Ulysses S. Grant, supervising the building of roads, bridges, and fortifications at the Siege of

Vicksburg. He then marched as an engineer with Sherman's troops through Georgia and was present at the burning of Atlanta. Later, at the elegant dinner parties he and his wife often hosted in Chicago, Jenney sometimes recalled his experience in the army engineering corps. It was, he said, "an excellent school" for learning to solve difficult problems in construction. The first telling of the birdcage story may also have been heard at the dinner table of one of these parties.

There were already a number of tall buildings in the Loop by the time Major Jenney began the Home Insurance Building in 1883, and nine more were under construction in the neighborhood. The crowding of tall buildings close together created a new problem. Even with the assistance of iron framework, the taller the building, the thicker the supporting walls of its lowest floors had to be. As electric light was not yet in use, the most desirable commercial spaces on the first and second floors could only be gloomily lit caves deep in the canyons created by a forest of tall buildings. When Jenney was hired by the New York Home Insurance Company to design their Chicago headquarters, his assignment was not necessarily to build an exceptionally tall building. His primary challenge was to build one that could have almost as much rentable space and daylight in the first floor areas as it did in the upper floors.

The great cathedrals of the Middle Ages were, of course, tall masonry structures, with no iron support, that admitted ample daylight to their lower areas. Their spires were much taller than anything Jenney would build. Chartres in France is 375 feet, Salisbury, the tallest in England, is 404 feet, and Cologne Cathedral in Germany is 515 feet. Their high vaulted interiors do not, however, have intervening floors that cut off the light before it reaches the ground. Furthermore, wherever windows interrupt cathedral walls, the missing support has to be replaced with massive buttresses of masonry between windows. The ground area or "footprint" of such a support system takes up far too much space to be considered for a commercial building on a piece of valuable real estate in the middle of a crowded city. Louis H. Sullivan

A Gothic interior. The design of magnificent Gothic churches was not suited for commercial buildings in terms of light and space.

summed up the problem of the tall masonry office building. "Not only did its thick walls entail the loss of space," commented Sullivan, "but its unavoidably small window openings could not furnish the . . . desirable ratio of glass area to rentable floor area."

Thomas Edison patented the incandescent lightbulb in 1879, and in 1882 in New York City, he completed the first electric power plant. But in Chicago electric light was not yet an option. Admitting daylight, not to mention fresh air, to the lower floors of tall buildings was still a baffling problem. Jenney solved this problem by inventing a new type of structure. He began the Home Insurance Building with iron and masonry support for the lower floors. The iron was like the systems used earlier in New York, and the masonry was partly to protect the iron from the intense heat of a fire. Not long after the building was begun, an innovation rolled into town. It was a new type of steel I-beam that had been developed by the Carnegie-Phipps company in Pittsburgh.

The Home Insurance Building, now demolished, was the first with steel in its frame. Ghostly pedestrians on the sidewalk indicate that this photo was taken with a fairly long time exposure.

Steel, an iron alloy containing tiny amounts of carbon and other elements, had, of course, been around for centuries. Its strength and lightness compared to plain iron made it suitable for such items as swords and suits of armor, but it was too expensive to be used in large quantities as a structural material. In the mid-nineteenth century the British metallurgist Sir Henry Bessemer invented a method of manufacturing good-quality steel in substantial quantities. By 1865 the Bessemer process was being used in Chicago for the production of railroad rails, but no one had yet tried this kind of steel in construction. When the first trainload of Carnegie-Phipps steel arrived in Chicago, the local salesman persuaded Jenney that the product would be lighter and stronger in construction than wrought iron. The fact that it was also relatively inexpensive aided Jenney in persuading his clients to accept a change in construction plan. As a result, the Home Insurance Building was given a steel skeleton above the sixth floor, a feature that helped revolutionize the building of skyscrapers.

The idea for a lighter nonmasonry structure probably came to Jenney from several sources. Chicago historian Donald Miller suggests it is possible that he got it from the cagelike wooden balloon-frame houses first developed in the city. If wooden support systems were models, however, Jenney's steel cage owes somewhat more to the ancient post-and-beam construction that preceded balloon framing. Other historians say that the typhoon-proof bamboo-frame huts Jenney saw in the Philippines may have influenced him. In addition, Jenney's bridge-building experience in the Civil War must have increased his knowledge of the possibilities of metal structures. Whatever his inspiration, Jenney's new system meant that it was no longer necessary to rely on masonry for support. Outer walls could now have enormous windows, even at ground level. Since these walls were no longer needed for support, they might be made entirely of glass. The only limitation was the technology of making huge sheets of glass.

As a material for luxury items, such as beads and perfume bottles, glass has been around since ancient times. In the sixteenth, seventeenth,

Three decades after the innovative use of structural steel in Chicago, New York's Woolworth Building demonstrated how much William Jenney's concept had revolutionized the construction industry.

and eighteenth centuries, glass makers developed ways of making flat pieces from blown glass to use as window panes. The size of these panes was limited by the lung capacity of the glass blowers who made them. In the nineteenth century manufacturers in Europe and the United States began experimenting with methods of passing molten glass through rollers to make much larger sheets. In the 1890s the newest developments in this technology made it possible to cover large window openings with plate glass, as Daniel Burnham did with his Reliance Building. One writer called it "a glass tower" because its walls had more glass than stone. In 1891 Jenney also used plate glass windows in a department store known as the Second Leiter Building. In this structure the granite columns that separate grids of large windows echo the steel framework of the building.

Because of his innovative use of steel, some historians have hailed William Jenney as the architect of the first modern skyscraper. Others say that a Minneapolis architect named LeRoy S. Buffington actually had the idea first, unbeknownst to Jenney. Still others downgrade his achievement as unartistic. Historian Thomas Hines describes the Home Insurance Building as "a dowdy 'stacking' of floors atop one another. It failed to achieve even the aesthetic success of Root and Burnham's earlier wall-supported Montauk." Nevertheless, the innovation was now a reality, and Hines at least gives credit for that. "Burnham and Root were quick to sense the importance of Jenney's accomplishment, and their handsome ten-story, Rand-McNally Building . . . was the first tall building in the world to be completely supported by an all-steel frame." The Rand-McNally Building, completed in 1890, was also significant because it brought natural light into the building by means of an interior courtyard.

The inner courtyard idea had been tried by Burnham and Root two years earlier in a curiosity called the Rookery. The building took its name from the structure that had previously occupied the location. Immediately after the Great Fire, a temporary city hall was slapped up at Adams and LaSalle Streets. The rather seedy neighborhood was a major roosting place for flocks of pigeons and crows. Soon crooked politicians "roosted" there also, like rowdy crows or rooks. Chicagoans nicknamed the place the Rookery. Despite the name, the work spaces are comfortable. Over the years many well-known architects have designed interior renovations for the Rookery, and today it is still a prestigious address for business offices.

Another effort by Burnham and Root to admit extra light to the interior of a building was the Women's Temple at Monroe and LaSalle Streets. Completed in 1892, it had a footprint in the form of an H, thus creating two inner courtyards. It also had an articulated facade with

Above: The interior lobby of the Rookery admitted daylight before electricity came into common use.

*Right:
The Rookery, LaSalle Street, Chicago, built in 1888, is still a sought-after business address.*

The Women's Temple, designed by Burnham and Root, was commissioned by WCTU in honor of its founder, Frances Willard.

towers at the corners and a sloping turreted roof like some of the mansions the architects had designed earlier. The building was commissioned by the Women's Christian Temperance Union (WCTU) to honor one of its founders, Frances Willard, an early campaigner for votes for women.

Burnham and Root had become one of the best-known architectural firms in Chicago. They were also developing a national reputation and became involved in an idea that began to take form in several cities around the country. The intention was to celebrate the centennial of the adoption of the United States Constitution and the four-hundredth anniversary of the discovery of America by Christopher Columbus. New York, St. Louis, Washington, D. C., and Chicago all wanted to link the two anniversaries with an extravagant three-year-long world's fair. In 1889 Mayor DeWitt Cregier appointed a committee of two hundred and fifty leading citizens to lobby Congress to award Chicago the honor of being host city. The main argument was that as a major railroad hub located near the middle of the country, Chicago could offer the most convenient access to the fair for the greatest number of citizens. In 1890 President Benjamin Harrison signed an act of Congress authorizing Chicago as the host of an "international exhibition" of art and industry. Then the political jockeying moved from Washington to Chicago itself.

Park designers Frederick Law Olmsted and his associate, Henry Codman, were invited to come from New York and help pick the site for the fair. After some tense discussions within the corporation that was raising the money, Jackson Park, a six-hundred-acre undeveloped area in the southern part of the city along the shore of Lake Michigan,

Best known for designing Central Park in New York, Frederick Law Olmsted helped choose and landscape the site of the World's Columbian Exposition in Chicago.

was selected. Olmsted and Codman were then appointed as consulting landscape architects by the directors of the corporation. Burnham and Root were appointed consulting architects, and later Burnham, called "Uncle Dan" by his colleagues, was given the position of chief of construction. Early in January of 1891, John Root died unexpectedly, and the management of the enormous project fell entirely to Burnham. He had worked hard to put together a team of the nation's best architects from Chicago, New York, Boston, and Kansas City. When they met in February in the library of Burnham's mansion to share plans for the various buildings, the famous sculptor Augustus Saint-Gaudens was

American sculptor Augustus Saint-Gaudens, educated at the Ecole des Beaux-Arts in Paris, helped plan the World's Columbian Exposition.

present as an artistic consultant. At the end of the meeting, he came to Burnham and said, "This is the greatest meeting of artists since the fifteenth century."

There were, in fact, some outstandingly creative people present and a number of others who became well known as the Exposition faded into history. From New York, George B. Post would design the Manufactures and Liberal Arts Building. Two other New York firms that won projects were Richard Hunt for the Central Administration Building, and McKim, Mead, and White for the Agriculture Building. Peabody and Stearns of Boston were assigned the Machinery Building, and Van Brunt and Howe of Kansas City the Electricity Building. From Chicago, Adler and Sullivan would design the Transportation Building, and Jenney and Mundie the Horticulture Building. Daniel Burnham would be responsible for the actual construction and final appearance of the magnificent endeavor. It was an astonishing collection of talent. Perhaps the most striking thing is that a vast but temporary collection of edifices of wood and painted plaster was to be designed mostly by architects who were already involved in very busy offices elsewhere. They took time out from their demanding and lucrative careers to participate in a truly remarkable national production.

Many historians have claimed that the fair was a negative development. Louis H. Sullivan, despite his Transportation Building, said later that the fair's neoclassical style, echoing ancient Greece and Rome, was "an appalling calamity" for the development of an American style. This view has been argued for and against in the twentieth century. It is, however, an issue of taste, a dispute that is never settled.

Methods of building are a different matter. In 1893 they were in the middle of an enormous change that reflected the national experience. Throughout the nineteenth century the United States had been in the process of a major shift from its traditionally rural way of life. It was becoming an industrialized society centered in its cities. Putting cities together and then pulling them apart in order to put them together again to meet new technologies is more complex than country living.

Main canal of the World's Columbian Exposition, also known as the Chicago World's Fair

Saint-Gaudens may have exaggerated in comparing the designers of the World's Columbian Exposition to artists of the European Renaissance in the fifteenth century. Nevertheless, he had identified the huge significance of the planning meeting that took place in Burnham's library. None of the buildings at the Columbian Exposition could be called skyscrapers, but the whole event had a lasting impact on American architecture. Building in the city had become a collaborative business requiring the careful cooperation of urban planners, architects, structural engineers, mechanical engineers, building contractors, and skilled laborers. Such a grand collaboration took place at the World's Columbian Exposition in Chicago. It was the sort of team effort that would be repeated and refined in the next century with the styles and shapes of skyscrapers.

A decorative carving in the lobby of his own building
shows Frank W. Woolworth counting coins.
In 1910 he asked his architect, Cass Gilbert,
to create the tallest building in the world.
The Woolworth Building held that record until 1930.

CHAPTER FIVE

NEW YORK SHOWS OFF

Daniel Burnham referred to the out-of-town architects who gathered in his library to discuss the drawings for the World's Columbian Exposition buildings as "the Beaux-Arts Boys." He was just kidding. Burnham himself had selected the group, and he would not have invited anyone to design for the fair whose work he did not respect. The curious nickname referred to a specific style. Most of the architects from the East Coast had studied at the famous Ecole des Beaux-Arts in Paris, where they had learned to appreciate architectural styles and decorative features of the past. Their designs usually reflected the styles of ancient Greece and Rome, the Gothic cathedrals of the Middle Ages, and the palaces of the Italian Renaissance.

Louis H. Sullivan, one of the few Beaux-Arts-trained Chicagoans, eventually rebelled against the tradition. Although he continued to appreciate decoration, he felt that the outer form of a building should reveal the inside structure. On the facade of his only building in New York, the decorative columns of the exterior run almost the full height

The masonry on the facade of the Bayard-Condict Building echoes the steel skeleton that supports it. This is the only example of Chicago style in New York City designed by Louis H. Sullivan.

of the facade. These do not add any strength to the building, but they echo the interior steel columns that support the structure. "The Bayard-Condict Building tells us how it is constructed," writes Eric Nash in *New York's 50 Best Skyscrapers.* Tucked away in the less-traveled streets of downtown Manhattan, it is a lone example in New York of what came to be called the Chicago School.

Most architects of the Chicago School were trained as engineers rather than artists. Burnham and Root, often encouraged by their sometime employer, Peter Brooks, had produced buildings that looked plainer than the more artistic structures then found in eastern cities. It seems odd, therefore, that one of Burnham's best-known later buildings is the Fuller Building, an innovative Beaux-Arts structure which is still a well-known landmark in modern New York.

The Fuller Building, finished in 1903, is better known by another name. At the turn of the century, electric irons had not been invented. The family laundry was smoothed with a device called a flatiron, a thick and heavy triangular-shaped piece of iron that was heated on the top of a cast-iron coal stove. Confined to its narrow triangular lot, the Fuller Building resembled one of those household items, and New Yorkers soon nicknamed it the Flatiron.

The original name came from the company that built it. The George A. Fuller Company was a general contractor in the business of organizing the materials, subcontractors, and work schedules of large urban construction projects. This was a growing role, separate from that of the architectural firm. Because tall buildings were becoming such a complex business, it seemed necessary to separate the functions of design and construction. The company maintained an office in the Flatiron until 1929, when it moved its headquarters uptown to a new Fuller Building. Throughout the twentieth century the George A. Fuller Company managed the construction of buildings all over the world. In New York three of its most important landmarks are the Plaza Hotel, Lever House, and the Seagram Building.

The Fuller Company was founded in Chicago in 1882. This may be why Burnham's firm was selected to design the Flatiron, but it is most unlikely that he, personally, would have decided on a Beaux-Arts facade. After the World's Columbian Exposition, Burnham's company had become nationally famous for urban planning. "Burnham himself did no architectural designing," Landau and Condit state in their book on New York skyscrapers, "and it is difficult to say who in his large office actually designed the Flatiron." Whoever did created a unique sample of the Beaux-Arts Style at Broadway and Fifth Avenue.

The walls resemble an Italian Renaissance palace, the first three floors of coarse limestone giving visual weight to the lower portion of the building. The next thirteen stories have windows grouped in twos

Left: The view of the Flatiron from uptown that reminded Stieglitz of an ocean liner

Below: At the third story the limestone of the Flatiron Building shifts from a heavy style to a lighter one with delicately carved decoration.

with carved decoration in between, including geometric patterns and classical images. The top stories, decorated with columns and arches, are crowned with an ornamental cornice.

The Flatiron reveals nothing of its internal structure, which was actually one of the first steel frames in New York. The Jenney-type cage was innovative in its additional bracing for extra strength against high winds. Because the building was so narrow, New Yorkers watching the construction bet on how far away carved stones from the cornice would land when it blew over in the first bad storm. This slenderness also excited the famous photographer Alfred Stieglitz. After viewing the narrow uptown corner, he said the Flatiron was "like the bow of a monster ocean steamer—a picture of new America still in the making."

Just across Madison Square Park from the Flatiron, the spirit of Beaux Arts lived on when a seven-hundred-foot tower was added to the building belonging to the Metropolitan Life Insurance Company. In the later years of the nineteenth century, MetLife had, says Judith Dupré in *Skyscrapers,* "pioneered insurance sales to immigrant wage earners whose death could mean destitution to their families." By 1907 it claimed to have sold more life insurance "than all the other New York companies combined." Its president, John Rogers Hegeman, decided the company needed an impressive building and hired the firm of Napoleon LeBrun and Company to design an imposing tower for the existing headquarters.

Modeled after the famous bell tower of St. Mark's Square in Venice, the MetLife tower rested on concrete pilings that were sunk thirty to forty feet below street level to Manhattan's bedrock. These piers and the steel framing they supported represented the best in a technology that was becoming standardized. With refinements and improvements, it would serve the construction industry into the building boom of the 1920s and beyond. The tower's fifty floors were served by high-speed electric elevators made by the Otis Company. The marble-clad frame supported the world's largest four-faced clock, with Renaissance floral designs carved in the stonework around each face. To make sure that

Left: The MetLife Tower has the world's largest four-faced clock.

Right: The bell tower of St. Mark's Square in Venice was the model for the MetLife Tower.

no one missed the importance of MetLife, the tower was built twice as big as its ancestor in Italy.

For four years the Metropolitan Life Insurance Tower was the tallest building in the world. In 1913 it lost that title to another monument to a colossal ego. Frank W. Woolworth told his architect, Cass Gilbert, that he wanted a tower fifty feet higher than the MetLife. Opening his first five-and-ten-cent store in 1879, Woolworth built up a chain of six hundred retail stores by 1910. His fortune had become so immense that he could afford to pay cash for his ambitious new skyscraper, and he wanted Gilbert to use the Gothic lines of England's Houses of Parliament in London as inspiration.

F. W. Woolworth intended to impress the world. As one construction company executive remarked, "Beyond a doubt his ego was a thing of extraordinary size." Nevertheless, he still had one eye on making money. The restaurant and swimming pool in the basement were not only for show. They were to help attract well-heeled commercial tenants such as "lawyers, financial institutions, and high-class businesses" willing to pay substantial rents for impressive offices.

The "perpendicular" Gothic style of fifteenth-century England lends itself to Louis H. Sullivan's concept of a tall building's appearance. The soaring vertical lines of the terra-cotta tiles on the Woolworth's facade follow what the building's engineer called "the lines of strength" in the steel frame. This upward thrust is decorated with carved Gothic spires, arches, gargoyles, and other mythical creatures. Twentieth-century "mythical" creatures appear in carvings in the lobby, including one of Cass Gilbert contemplating a model of the building, and another of F. W. Woolworth himself, counting a stack of nickels. The whimsical decoration does not, however, diminish the total effect of the building with its tower that is nearly double the height of Salisbury Cathedral in England. In fact, at its grand opening, the colossal office building inspired the Reverend S. Parkes Cadman to call it a "Cathedral of Commerce."

The imposing size was breathtaking, but it also aroused criticism. In an engineering magazine, one unhappy writer complained that there was

F. W. Woolworth instructed his architect to use the "perpendicular" Gothic style of fifteenth-century England for his "Cathedral of Commerce."

no excuse "for the rearing of this great pile." He said that it would over-shadow nearby buildings and darken the streets. In addition, he predicted that its "population of several thousand people . . . will add another heavy burden to the transportation facilities." These problems were rather over-stated, but they foreshadowed some serious concerns of the future.

The construction industry of New York had come to a crisis. Very tall buildings might indeed create poor conditions for their immediate surroundings. A building built nine-hundred feet straight up from the very edges of its lot could be a huge and gloomy block casting a vast shadow over smaller buildings in the neighborhood. In fact, the New Equitable Building finished in 1915 was just such a building. People watching the construction became concerned that if others like it went up in the neighborhood, the streets would become dark and congested. In 1916 a new building code was adopted for the city that restricted how many feet a building could rise straight up from the sidewalk. At a certain height, perhaps ten floors up, it must have a "setback" from the lot line, and at higher levels it must step back again. A structure such as the 1926 Barclay-Vesey Building might look like a mixed col-

The Barclay-Vesey Building makes use of setbacks according to the 1916 New York Building Code.

lection of shorter buildings clustered around a tower, but new skyscrapers would be surrounded by ample sunlight and airspace.

Happily, the restrictions of the building code did not limit the application to architecture of a new style. This was a sleek machine-age look for all sorts of fashionable consumer goods from electric toasters to shiny automobiles. When Henry Ford introduced mass-production factory methods in 1914, annual car sales started to climb rapidly. In the 1920s General Motors began to stimulate car sales even more by introducing newly designed models every year. In 1925 the Exposition Internationale des Arts Decoratifs (International Exposition of Decorative Arts) took place in Paris. It celebrated the new style, now called Art Deco, that spoke to the world in a language of slender forms with smooth curved surfaces and simple geometric patterns. In 1930 this language reached a peak of expression in the Chrysler Building.

Walter P. Chrysler began his working career as a machinist's apprentice. In a few years he left the labor force for management, eventually becoming a vice president at General Motors, and in 1924 he began producing his own cars. In an amazingly short time, the Chrysler Corporation became one of the biggest auto makers in the United States. The achievement seemed to call for a showy new corporate headquarters. Walter P. Chrysler, like F. W. Woolworth before him, decided to trumpet his commercial success to the world by building a flamboyant New York skyscraper.

In compliance with the 1916 building code, the Chrysler Building's lower floors form a base shaped with four setbacks. The huge black granite entrances are a sharp contrast to the white ceramic brickwork of the facades, which are topped with horizontal lines of brick hubcaps. The soaring tower has setbacks of its own, and the corners are decorated with giant replicas of Chrysler and Plymouth hood ornaments. The tower is crowned on all four sides with six arches, each set with triangular windows. The crown is sheathed in a nickel and steel alloy that gleams in the sunshine, and the lighted edges of the triangular windows accentuate it at night. But this is not the end of the story.

Left: The Chrysler Building complied with the 1916 Building Code rules on setbacks.

Below: The mast on top of the Chrysler Building was secretly constructed inside the Art Deco tower and then hoisted up to make the building the world's tallest at the time.

William Van Alen, the Chrysler's architect, seems to have had an ego the equal of his employer. He was in a crazy and personal race with his rival and former partner, H. Craig Severance, for the tallest building in the world. While Severance was completing his 1,046-foot Bank of Manhattan Building on Wall Street, Van Alen was having a spire secretly built inside the Chrysler's tower. When it was pulled through the top of the tower, the spire made the Chrysler Building the world's tallest at 1,048 feet. Van Alen's surprise ending was a gloriously theatrical curtain call.

In early February 1930, while the Chrysler Building was still rising, jackhammers, power shovels, and sixteen-ton cranes were excavating a gigantic hole in the ground at Fifth Avenue at 34th Street. During March support columns were created by pouring 3,744 cubic yards of concrete into 210 holes that reached to Manhattan's bedrock thirty and forty feet beneath the bottom of the excavation. By mid-May steel-workers were bolting together a story a day on the framework that would soon support the Empire State Building. When it opened the following May, this colossal project of the construction firm Starrett Bros. and Eken, Inc. was the world's tallest skyscraper, a title it would hold for forty years.

The originator of the project was a real estate developer named Floyd Brown whose intention was to build rental space for a money-making combination of shops and offices. The first calculations comparing building cost to annual income suggested that a highly profitable plan might be to build a structure of fifty floors. Then Brown's financiers did some additional calculations and concluded that a building of seventy-five to eighty floors would prove even more profitable. Another five or ten stories could easily top the Chrysler's spire. The additional floors would require the added expense of another bank of elevators, but the prestige of having an office in the world's tallest building might make it more attractive to renters. The decision to go for a world-class sky-scraper would soon prove to be a world-class miscalculation.

The original planning took place in 1928, but by the time the 210 concrete piers were sunk to the city's bedrock, the worldwide economic

A bolter working on the Empire State's frame at the fifty-second floor. On construction sites in the 1930s, workers did not wear hard hats.

catastrophe of the 1930s had begun. The Great Depression severely limited the building industry and caused the Empire State Building's directors to impose economies on their project. They wanted to minimize their losses in mortgage payments and taxes on real estate that was not yet a profit-making business. The frame was completed in the record time of four months, and the gray Indiana limestone that encased it was less expensive to install than other materials. The only place where extra money was spent was on the Art Deco crown of aluminum and stainless steel, with its tall mast on top intended as an anchorage for dirigible blimps. It turned out that high winds made it impossible to moor blimps safely, and the tragic flaming crash of the Hindenburg in New Jersey in 1936 put an end to commercial travel by blimp.

So that the two or three thousand skilled laborers and tradesmen working on high would not spend valuable time coming down for lunch, it was brought to them at their job sites on the various floors. The high-pressure schedule of construction may have saved money, but there was a human cost. More than a few workers died on the job, including one killed in blasting for the foundation, another who slipped off the framework, and yet another who fell down an elevator shaft.

To the great pride of the workforce, as well as the satisfaction of the developers, the Empire State Building was completed under budget and ahead of schedule. Its official opening was a major publicity event, but barely 30 percent of the space had been rented. Clever New Yorkers nicknamed it "the Empty State Building." Throughout the 1930s it was only the enthusiasm of tourists flocking to marvel at the building itself and paying to gaze at Brooklyn, Manhattan, and New Jersey from the observation deck that kept it from bankruptcy.

In 1933 the Empire State Building made a cameo appearance in the original version of *King Kong*. At the end of the film, the giant ape teeters on the crown of the building, clutching the heroine in his fist while fighting off a cloud of fighter planes. The building also has supporting roles in many other films, among them, *The Moon is Blue, An Affair to Remember,* and *Sleepless in Seattle.* In 1945 it made sensational news one foggy Saturday morning when a B-25 bomber crashed into the seventy-ninth floor, killing fourteen people. More would have died if it had been a workday. The repairs took almost as long as the original construction, but the building survived, and finally, in 1950, the business showed a profit. In the history of architecture, the Empire State Building stands as the last great building of the skyscraper boom of the 1920s.

*Left: Workers rig large
canvases on the
Empire State Building
as temporary cover for
the damage caused by
a bomber crashing into
the seventy-ninth floor.*

*Right: Old movie poster
of* King Kong *seated at the
base of the Empire State's
crowning tower while
holding the heroine and
grabbing a fighter plane*

When it was finished in 1931, the Empire State Building was the tallest in the world and remained so for forty years.

Today the building attracts twice as many tourists as the much taller World Trade Center downtown. Perhaps its midtown location is more convenient, or maybe visitors find the Art Deco profile prettier than the huge glass and aluminum boxes of the twin towers. Whatever the reasons, Eric Nash in *New York's 50 Best Skyscrapers* says, "The Empire State Building is the best known skyscraper in the world, as immediately recognizable as the Eiffel Tower or the Taj Mahal."

*The twin towers of the World Trade Center are a colossal
example of the International Style.*

CHAPTER SIX

OUTSIDE INSIDE

Chicago and New York were the incubators of the modern skyscraper. Although this American invention appears in cities around the world, the majority of its technical developments were born in these two cities. One such development was the idea of a city-within-a-city that appeared on the New York scene in 1940.

This city-within-a-city began in 1931 and originated with John D. Rockefeller, Jr., whose father founded the vast Rockefeller family fortune. Three major architectural firms were needed to design the buildings. A partner in one of these firms, Raymond Hood, who had studied at MIT and the Ecole des Beaux-Arts, was the mastermind. He became the general of a small army of people who drew the blueprints for the Rockefeller project. Computer-aided design for architecture was still years in the future, so architects had to draw all their plans by hand at adjustable drafting tables or drawing boards. There is a story that once, when Hood became worried that his plans were running behind schedule, he ordered a supervisor to hire an additional draftsman. He was informed this could not be done because there were already too many people working in the drafting room. Hood said to hire another person anyway. "There's always one guy on the can," he growled.

The project, Rockefeller Center, is a group of tall buildings clustered around a seventy-story skyscraper, still called the RCA Building by many New Yorkers, even though it has had other owners since 1940. Viewed from the east or west, the RCA, now the General Electric Building, looks like a slender tower. Viewed from uptown or downtown, it looks like a giant slab, foreshadowing some of the architecture that was to appear just after World War II.

More significant than the RCA's varied profiles, however, was a utility that office workers now take for granted. Air-conditioning had been used in factories since about 1900, but it had not been seriously tried in office buildings until Rockefeller Center. Previously offices had to be placed along the exterior wall of a building in order to have at least one window for ventilation. The innovation of air-conditioned office buildings would change forever the way architects thought about office space.

Even more impressive than the master scheme of offices, however, is the layout of restaurants, broadcasting studios, and two hundred shops linked together with landscaping and artwork. The outdoor centerpiece for all of this was not part of the original design. In the middle of the complex, there was meant to be an ornate subway entrance with a statue of the mythical hero Prometheus flying above it. For a number of reasons, it could not be built, but the solution to the problem looks as though it was always intended. Instead of a hole, there is now a flat surface that is filled with umbrella-shaded tables for an outdoor cafe in warmer weather and cleared for use as an ice-skating rink when the weather turns cold. In the holiday season a huge Christmas tree towers over the rink.

Thousands of tourists visit Rockefeller Center every year for holiday shopping and a visit to Radio City Music Hall, the city's largest movie theatre, to see holiday shows and dance revues featuring the

Left: Rockefeller Center, with the RCA, or GE, Building viewed from the northeast and the Hudson River in the background. Sculpture of Prometheus is just visible below the main entrance.

Below: Sculpture of Prometheus presides over the plaza that is an outdoor café in summer and an ice-skating rink in winter.

world-famous Rockettes. Rockefeller Center welcomes people into a gleaming urban miniworld. It leaves the harsher aspects of city life outside and brings the happier features inside.

Another way of separating the outside from the inside is to put a glass wall between the two. After World War II this began to happen in skyscrapers of a new style that came from Europe. At meetings in London during 1946, the first General Assembly of the United Nations decided to build its permanent headquarters on land along the East River in Manhattan. The office building, completed in 1952, is a tall glass slab called the United Nations Secretariat. The slab is only 72 feet

The U.N. Secretariat is one of the earliest examples of the International Style. This view from the East River shows the Empire State and the Chrysler buildings flanking the Secretariat, with the low curving roofline of the General Assembly Building to the right near the water.

thick, but its blue-green tinted walls are 287 feet wide by 544 feet high. Beside it, the low solid walls of the General Assembly Building are hardly noticeable.

The main consultant to the international group that designed the project was a Swiss-born architect named Le Corbusier. His colleagues sometimes referred to him as "Corbu," but his real name was Charles Édouard Jeanneret. Le Corbusier's work was strongly influenced by the Bauhaus, a school of design that had started in Germany in 1919 and was headed first by Walter Gropius and then, in 1928, by Ludwig Mies van der Rohe. In 1933 the Nazis closed the Bauhaus, driving many of its teachers to the United States.

Strict simplicity is the hallmark of the Bauhaus Style, and the designer's work must reflect the nature of the materials used. In architecture it is called the International Style, and it takes Louis H. Sullivan's ideas of form and function to a sparse extreme. The crisp thin lines of a Bauhaus structure make the clean lines of a Sullivan facade seem like romantic gingerbread.

Earlier in the century one of Sullivan's students, Frank Lloyd Wright, had emerged as America's premier architect, but in the 1950s his Prairie Style was totally eclipsed by the International Style. In the

Frank Lloyd Wright working with architecture students

same year that the United Nations Secretariat was completed, a more artistic example of the International Style opened in midtown Manhattan. Lever House, designed by the Chicago-based firm of Skidmore, Owings and Merrill (SOM), is only twenty-four stories high, leading some people to say it is not a true skyscraper. Nevertheless, the corporate American headquarters of the British manufacturer of Lifebuoy soap and Tide laundry detergent is definitely a structure in the International Style. The simplicity of its horizontal unit floating on square stainless steel columns and the clear blue-green of the sheer glass walls of its slab-shaped tower are elements that were too often copied in cities everywhere.

Lever House is an International Style glass box above a horizontal glass box.

The glass box simplicity of the International Style had a parallel in the art, music, and interior design of the 1960s. It was known as minimalism, and its philosophy was perhaps best expressed by Ludwig Mies van der Rohe. Mies had fled Hitler's Germany and come to Chicago as dean of architecture at the Armour Institute, now the Illinois Institute of Technology. "Less is more," said Mies, inspiring forests of starkly simple buildings featuring squared-off profiles with severely restrained color and decoration.

"Less is more expensive," might have been the revised slogan when Mies van der Rohe and Philip Johnson set out to design the austere but elegant Seagram Building on Park Avenue in New York. All the different setbacks that are required to set the mass of a building back from

Ludwig Mies van der Rohe, who fled Nazi Germany in 1933 and became an influential American architect, is shown here with a model of his Crown Building, College of Architecture, Illinois Institute of Technology.

76

The elegant Seagram Building is one of the finest examples of the International Style.

the sidewalk are combined at ground level into one vast granite plaza with two decorative pools. A standard steel skeleton rises thirty-eight stories above an arcade and supports an exterior of custom-tinted brown glass and hand-cast decorative bronze I-beams that echo the upward thrust of the interior steel. Added to the initial high cost of the materials is the expensive upkeep of the Seagram's bronze exterior, which must be oiled by hand every year to maintain the warm brown tones. "Mies believed," says one skyscraper historian, "that in an otherwise severe style the decoration should be supplied by the richness of the materials."

Mies always thought the Seagram Building represented his very best work, but it spawned a rash of cheap imitations across the country. Glass box architecture began to earn a remarkable amount of negative criticism, not only from the general public but from professionals as well. "Less is only more," said Frank Lloyd Wright, "where more is no good." A harsher evaluation was made by a Yale architect named Robert Venturi, who commented, "Less is a bore."

As the International Style was revising the look of skyscrapers in the 1960s, the methods of supporting tall buildings were revolutionized by an engineer at Skidmore, Owings and Merrill. Although he worked in Chicago, Fazlur Khan was born in East Bengal, a province of British colonial India that is now Bangladesh. After earning a degree in engineering at the University of Dhaka in Bangladesh, Khan came to the United States to do advanced work in structural engineering at the University of Illinois, Urbana-Champaign. In 1955 he joined SOM and eventually started using computers to find new ways to make tall buildings wind-resistant.

The system that Khan finally devised was the frame-tube structure. The word "tube" can be misleading because it usually refers to a hollow cylinder such as a water pipe. In the case of Khan's invention, the hollow tube is square. Instead of having continuous walls like a pipe, its sides are a framework of steel. One way of understanding the system is to imagine that Khan turned the conventional steel frame inside out. There are no internal support columns in a simple tube-structure building. All the supporting framework is external.

A tube stuck in the ground can withstand a good deal of wind. A square frame tube standing upright is also wind-resistant. In the case of SOM's John Hancock Center in Chicago, the frame tube was given extra strength by means of diagonal bracing on the face of the frame. The giant Xs that tie one corner of the building to another may seem like decoration, but they are really an important part of the structure. They transfer some of the pressure of the wind on the windward side of the building to the opposite side. Even more strength was given the building by tapering its sides gradually upward for its entire 1,127 feet.

Left: The John Hancock Center as seen from the street

Below: "Big John" is a major presence on the Chicago skyline.

This makes the building seem like a giant descendant of the small galvanized steel towers that were erected on prairie farms to support windmills for pumping water before rural electrification.

In addition to designing an innovative building, Khan and his SOM teammate, Bruce Graham, modified a concept from the recent past. The John Hancock Center, like Rockefeller Center, is a city-within-a-city. It combines spaces for shops, offices, condominiums, and all the support services for these functions in one location. A person lucky enough to own one of the condominiums and have a job in one of the offices would never have to face the bone-chilling winds from Lake Michigan that make Chicago winters so painfully cold.

By the time the Hancock, nicknamed "Big John," opened in 1969, the giant retailing firm Sears, Roebuck and Company had decided to combine all their offices in a single corporate headquarters in Chicago. To manage the project, they hired the real estate development company Cushman and Wakefield who, in turn, selected SOM to design it. The firm then called upon its experienced team of Khan and Graham to manage the ambitious effort.

In response to the complex challenge, Fazlur Khan presented a variation on the frame-tube idea. If a single tube offered good resistance to the wind, then perhaps a bundle of tubes that supported each other would be even stronger. Khan designed nine tubes of varying heights tied together in a square. Each tube would be seventy-five feet on a side. The three tubes on each street side of the building would then be 225 feet, making the footprint of the building 50,000 square feet. Two corner tubes would rise only to fifty floors, leaving seven to rise an additional sixteen floors, where two more corner tubes would stop. The remaining five central tubes would rise to the ninetieth floor, and two of these would continue on to complete the building's one hundred and ten stories. The shorter tubes created setbacks in the total structure. Models of the design were tested in a wind tunnel at the University of Ontario, and the results appeared satisfactory, so Sears agreed to go ahead with the multimillion-dollar project.

Left: The Sears Tower as seen from the street

Below: The Sears Tower dwarfs other tall buildings in the Loop area of Chicago.

Even a huge corporation like Sears could not have afforded the mammoth building if it had been designed in the conventional way. A birdcage skeleton like Major Jenney's would have required twice as much structural steel as the tube system. Khan's design also used a newly developed higher-grade steel that was about two-thirds the weight of conventional steel, and it was put together with a new technology called fusion welding. Many sections of the steelwork were prefabricated elsewhere and then trucked into the city to the building site. During construction, work was stalled several times because of winds so strong workers could not stand up in them. That was to be expected in Chicago, but the design was economical and the construction methods were efficient. The city could anticipate the grandest state-of-the-art building ever to grace its skyline.

When Sears Tower, with its sleek skin of black aluminum and bronze-tinted glass, opened in 1974, however, a number of problems emerged. The huge numbers of people working in the building presented a traffic problem. Even with staggered business hours, some people needed as much as a half hour to get from street level to their offices. Once there, many workers found their modern surroundings cold and depressing. Worst of all, wind turned out to be a problem after all. The tubes seemed wind-resistant in the same way stalks of bamboo might be in a hurricane. They did not blow over but they swayed. The groaning of the building could be disturbing on the eightieth floor, and windows often cracked.

Tens of millions of dollars spent on renovations did not solve all the problems. Competition from K Mart and Wal-Mart had reduced Sears's share of the retail market, and in 1989 they moved their offices out of the city. The building was then put up for sale, and four buyers responded, but the final deal fell through at the last minute. In 1990 a real estate developer was hired to renovate the interior space and find new tenants. Today Sears no longer owns the building but it is still called the Sears Tower and it attracts many tourists.

The winds of Chicago may be legendary, but they are not the only ones to challenge design engineers. In 1977 the First National City Bank, later called Citibank and now Citigroup, opened a new corporate headquarters in New York. Thanks to the negotiations of St. Peter's Lutheran Church, which owned much of the real estate for the building site, Citicorp Center was intended to be a model for keeping huge buildings from imposing too much on city living. From the start the design requirements seemed challenging, but no one could have predicted how extremely troublesome they were to become because of wind problems.

The agreement with St. Peter's called for Citibank to build a new freestanding church for the congregation on the northwest corner of the block. Supported by four massive nine-story supercolumns, the building was to be a square-tube structure above the new church and a plaza with shops. These supercolumns presented a major design problem. If the church was to be on the corner of the site and the plaza open and welcoming, the columns could not be directly under each corner of the square tube.

The final design placed them under the center of each face of the building, with the corners cantilevered over open space. This decision created a difficult challenge for the consulting engineer, William LeMesurier. The weight of the frame tubes had to be supported at the corners somehow. LeMesurier designed diagonal girders or struts to be placed every eight stories. They would run from the corners to the centers of the facades and be welded to the frame. Wind tunnel tests indicated that this system would withstand once-in-a-century storms.

Even in normal conditions, however, the exceptionally lightweight frame-tube structure would sway in the wind. A four-hundred-ton concrete block called a tuned mass damper, the first of its kind, was mounted on a thin bed of oil one floor below the the sloping top of Citicorp Center. Whenever the wind causes the building to sway more than one foot per second, a computer tells the electric-powered damper which way to slide in order to counter each sway.

The slope-roofed floors above the damper were originally intended

Left: The Citicorp's massive support columns are located under the center of each facade instead of at the corners. This feature created unusual design problems for the steel skeleton.

Right: The Citicorp Center was the first skyscraper to have a tuned mass damper to reduce sway caused by the wind.

as a space for setback condominiums with terraces, but the zoning regulations did not permit residential use of the building. The roof was redesigned to accommodate collectors for solar energy, but the system did not prove to be cost-efficient at the time of construction. Architect Hugh Stubbins decided to keep the unusual roofline anyway and use the space inside to house air-conditioning equipment.

While Citicorp Center was under construction, the contractor decided that the ultrastrong, new-technology welding for the diagonal girders was too expensive, and instead, he fastened them to the frame with bolts. LeMesurier, who worked in Cambridge, Massachusetts, did not find out until later but calculated that the bolts would still be adequate to meet the requirements of the New York City building code. In those days the code requirements were based on tests that assumed the wind was blowing directly on only one wall of the building. In a graduate engineering class he was teaching at Harvard, LeMesurier used his design to set up a new problem for his students. It called for calculations assuming quartering winds, or winds approaching the corner of the building diagonally and putting pressure on two adjoining sides. The results of the problem showed that quartering winds of hurricane strength would put unacceptable pressure on the structure and could cause the building to collapse.

To eliminate the risk, the worried LeMesurier designed large steel "Band-Aids" to be welded over each bolted joint. Then building department officials and Citibank executives were informed. Each group understood the problem and authorized the repairs. Sections of wall were stripped to expose the joints, large plywood boxes were built around each work area, and the actual welding was done at night so that the noise would not disturb office workers. The next problem was how to inform the media without creating a panic. At that point LeMesurier's fears were put on hold by a newspaper strike.

The repairs were only partially completed, however, when a hurricane was reported moving north toward New York. The evacuation plan that had been established for the ten-block radius surrounding the building was put on alert. Then, to everyone's relief, the hurricane veered out to sea. LeMesurier's concerns for his career were also relieved. He had been afraid that other engineers would regard him as incompetent and that insurance people would see him as a bad risk. Fortunately for him, LeMesurier's insurance company was persuaded that, instead of trying to hide the danger, he had been up-front about a potential catastrophe. He had discovered an unexpected danger and worked hard to forestall a horrible disaster.

Today William LeMesurier's ghastly fears for the Citicorp Center are like the scary images of a nightmare banished by the light of dawn. The slant-topped building is a distinctive landmark on the New York skyline, and at street level the one-block site is a people-friendly space. A sunken plaza with public benches, an arcade with shops and restaurants, a convenient subway entrance, plus the church on the corner make up a small city-within-a-city. It is a pocket version of Rockefeller Center.

A century in Boston: Trinity Church, completed in 1877, is reflected in the glass wall of the John Hancock Tower, completed almost 100 years later.

CHAPTER SEVEN

ALL OVER THE WORLD

On a summer day in 1992, a young woman who worked in the John Hancock Tower in Boston started walking down sixty flights of stairs by the dim light of the emergency lamps. A junior executive who was a smoker at the time used his cigarette lighter to help reduce the gloom. As they descended, they were joined by other workers from lower floors. The main lights were off, and all the elevators were out of order. There was an electrical fire somewhere in the building. The only way for everyone to get out was to use the emergency exit stairs. For the young couple who started on the top floor, the hour-long ordeal was the beginning of a happy relationship. They started dating, eventually married, and now celebrate their anniversary by walking down all sixty floors of the Hancock Building and out into daylight at Copley Square.

In the technological jungle of the modern urban world, such happy endings do not happen very often. Indeed, the John Hancock had seemed like an aggressive monster from the day its plan was announced to the public in 1968. Many people objected that the building would dwarf the neighboring historic Trinity Church, designed by the famous architect H. H. Richardson. They were assured that the Hancock's outside walls, made entirely of huge panels of silvered glass, would actually emphasize the old church by reflecting its image to pedestrians in the parklike square.

Unfortunately, instead of enhancing a part of town Bostonians loved, the sixty-story mirror became an engineering nightmare. The heavy, five-by-eleven-foot, cool-tinted windows that paneled the exterior began to pop off the building's frame even before it was finished. For office workers inside the building, it was terrifying when a whole section of outer wall suddenly disappeared. For people on the sidewalks below, it was a heart-stopping experience when a sheet of glass the size of a large door crashed to the pavement. Each gaping hole in the facade was hastily covered with a sheet of plywood, and for a while the Hancock was known as the "Plywood Palace".

At first engineers suspected strong winds might be yanking the windows off the frame. Finally they discovered that the huge, custom-made, double-glazed panes, unlike any ever manufactured before, could not withstand extreme contrasts in temperature. When sunlight caused heat to build up inside the two sheets of a pane, tiny cracks developed, and any disturbance could then send the loosened panel crashing to the ground. In his biography of I. M. Pei, Michael Cannell explains that at the time engineering schools offered courses in the structural capabilities of materials such as steel and concrete. Glass, however, was not then considered structural. "There was no scientific way to test new windows except by trial and error," says Cannell. The faulty monstrosities were finally replaced with sturdy, single-pane windows made with glass similar to that used in fire doors.

After William LeMesurier had been called in to design a tuned mass damper to reduce the sway and the steel frame had been reinforced, the John Hancock Tower opened in 1976, five years behind schedule. Not only was it $50 million over budget, but up until 1981 additional millions would be spent on lawsuits and countersuits. Nevertheless, the architect, Henry N. Cobb of I. M. Pei and Partners, had included in his basically International Style design a modest hint of things to come. The north and south facades of the building are each split full-length by a triangular notch.

The triangular notch running from top to bottom makes the Hancock Tower a bit more than just another glass box.

While all the frustration and delay was going on in Boston, the massive twin towers of the World Trade Center rose up to dominate lower Manhattan with a final ponderous statement of the International Style. In San Francisco, however, the tyranny of the glass box was challenged by the elegant narrow spire of the earthquake-proof Transamerica Pyramid. Four years later, at about the time that the John Hancock Tower opened, another challenge to the International Style was completed in Atlanta, Georgia. The Peachtree Plaza Hotel has an outer skin of glass, but its shape is not a box. It is a seven-hundred-foot-tall cylinder.

The Transamerica Pyramid in San Francisco was a major step beyond the International Style.

In the 1980s many more new buildings were built with imaginative exteriors. A memorable innovation was created by Philip Johnson in New York with his AT&T building and its crown resembling a piece of antique Chippendale furniture. Some people said Johnson was making fun of the architectural establishment. Nevertheless, he went on to design the NationsBank Center in Houston, Texas, which had modern setbacks and Gothic lines reminiscent of the Woolworth Building.

Cobb and Pei also have work in Texas that mixes the International Style with new ideas. The First Interstate Bank Tower in Dallas has

The First Interstate Bank Tower in Dallas, Texas, is a multifaceted mirror.

glass curtain walls, but the roofline is a tall gable, and on one side there is a steep sloping triangular roof. The various geometric shapes combine to make a huge multifaceted mirror set against the Texas sky. More important than the imaginative shape is the public space beneath it, a plaza with a garden including many fountains and trees.

The hot sun also prompted imaginative designs when skyscrapers became an American export. In Jeddah, Saudi Arabia, Skidmore, Owings and Merrill designed the National Commercial Bank on a triangular footprint. The smooth, clean lines of the exterior would have delighted Mies van der Rohe, who died in 1969. Instead of a glass skin,

The National Commercial Bank in Jeddah, Saudi Arabia, is well designed to cope with the hot Arabian sun.

however, its exterior is covered entirely in Italian marble. The windows, banked inside huge "superwindows" cut in each facade, are well protected from the intense Arabian sun.

In the Far East tall buildings began to appear as economic development caused banks and corporations to seek larger headquarters that would also serve as showy company symbols. In Singapore the Overseas Union Bank hired a Japanese architect named Kenzo Tange to design a new skyscraper. Tange had first attracted international attention in 1949 with his Peace Center built at Hiroshima, the city that was destroyed by the first atomic bomb. He went on to design many public buildings in Japan, including a city hall for Tokyo in 1957 and the National Indoor Stadium for the Tokyo Olympics in 1964. In 1961 Tange founded an organization for urban planning and research called the Urbanists and Architects Team. It was modeled on a similar group, the Architects Collaborative, founded by Walter Gropius after he fled Germany in 1937 and became head of architecture at the Harvard School of Design. In 1986 Tange won the competition to design a brand-new Tokyo City Hall, which was completed in 1991.

Tange's nine-hundred-foot Overseas Union Bank is two triangular towers placed so close together that, from most points of view, they look like a single square building. The aluminum sides have groupings of twelve stories of windows interspersed by rows of tiny circular windows. At the base is a small park with shops and a subway entrance, and inside there are two six-story waterfalls. The quality of this public space springs from Tange's studies in traditional Japanese architecture. He incorporates these traditions into his modern designs but avoids literal interpretation, such as the Beaux-Arts Style of copying European features had done in America. Instead, Tange's approach is philosophical. His architectural concepts make use of traditional Japanese principles of restraint, simplicity, and visual openness.

The skyscraper may have been born and raised in America, but it has become a citizen of the world. Examples of this are two contrasting buildings, one in England and the other in Malaysia, that were designed by an American architect who was born and raised in Argentina. Cesar Pelli was educated at the University of Tucumán in Argentina, where he practiced and taught architecture briefly before coming to the United States for graduate studies at the University of Illinois. In 1954 he joined the firm of Finnish-American architect Eero Saarinen, serving as project designer for several important master-plans, most notably the TWA Terminal at John F. Kennedy International Airport. After ten years with Saarinen, Pelli spent many more with firms in Los Angeles and taught at the University of California School of Architecture. In 1977 he moved to New Haven, Connecticut, as Dean of the Graduate School of Architecture at Yale University. In the same year he also established his own firm, Pelli & Associates, and took on his first truly major commission, the expansion project of the Museum of Modern Art in New York. The MoMA expansion included an addition to the museum space as well as a residential tower that was to be Pelli's first skyscraper. At the age of fifty, Pelli had reached professional maturity.

An engineer who has worked with him says that unlike some architects, Pelli does not feel confined or frustrated by tight budgets, site restrictions, or a client's taste. Instead, he regards these as opportunities to be creative. Solving problems of budget, site, and taste is what architects are hired to do, and Pelli regards the solutions as art.

Another part of Pelli's philosophy is that buildings should not be monuments to the architect's ego. They should appear to be comfortable in their surroundings and offer a good quality of life for the people who will live and work in the settings the artist has designed. A small expression of this concept appears in the site-plan drawing for Canary Wharf Tower in London and the two other Pelli buildings included in an ambitious urban renewal master-plan by Skidmore, Owings and Merrill. Sketched alongside the footprints of Pelli's three buildings are the shadows they will cast.

Today the finished complex sits on the edge of the River Thames in a district known as Docklands. The area, which was badly bombed

The pyramid-topped Canary Wharf Tower is the anchor building for SOM's Docklands Project in London.

during World War II, used to be one of the toughest and scruffiest in London. The SOM plan was intended to link the economy of Great Britain to the rest of the world by building a corporate complex that would attract international investment bankers as tenants. Pelli's fifty-story, stainless steel, square tower, with its pyramid-shaped roof, seems rather solid and heavy. Perhaps his clients thought this was appropriate for a building that serves as the project's anchor.

In 1998 and eight thousand miles east of Canary Wharf Tower, a vastly more imaginative design by Pelli was completed in Kuala Lumpur, Malaysia. The Petronas Towers, the first of many gigantic skyscrapers in Asia, are the headquarters for the state-owned Malaysian oil company. The twin structures rise eighty-eight stories from two sixteen-sided geometric footprints. The windows on each story are shadowed from the tropical sun by overhanging horizontal bands of stainless steel, giving the outer surfaces a delicate ribbed appearance. As Islam is the national religion of Malaysia, there is a Muslim prayer room inside, oriented toward Mecca. Indeed, the two towers could serve as giant minarets from which muezzins might call Muslims to daily prayer.

"The symmetrical towers, joined with a bridge at the forty-second story, suggest a doorway," writes Judith Dupré. "For Pelli, it is this mys-

The Petronas Towers in Kuala Lumpur, Malaysia, form the gateway to a vast City Center.

terious void, not the record-breaking towers on either side, that gives Petronas Towers its unique identity." Pelli himself described the space as "a portal to the sky," and in this, his design fulfills one of its most important functions. Petronas Towers is intended to be the welcoming gateway to the brand new Kuala Lumpur City Center, a vast city-within-a-city and the brainchild of Prime Minister Mahathir Mohamad.

The Petronas Towers are more than a quarter of a mile high. There are even taller buildings going up in Asia, some of them designed by SOM. One of these, the Jin Mao Building in Shanghai, China, is designed to be 1,379 feet tall. A group of Chicago businessmen are planning a building in the Loop that they hope will reclaim for the city the title "The World's Tallest." Frank Lloyd Wright once designed a mile-high theoretical skyscraper. Modern engineering and architecture might someday make Wright's concept a reality.

Will that be a good idea? How tall is too tall? The original idea for the Empire State Building was fifty stories, but ultimately the planners doubled it. Fazlur Khan said "the technical man mustn't be lost in his own technology," yet the first Sears Tower office workers were emotionally lost, dehumanized in their own workplaces. The huge number of people coming and going in the Jin Mao Building poses a serious problem in traffic control around its base. Even with new technology, it is a challenge to make superskyscrapers that are people-friendly. High-speed express elevators make some people's ears pop, and ventilation systems in sealed buildings sometimes cause headaches and other allergic reactions. Although they may be restrained by tuned mass dampers, skyscrapers will sway on windy days, causing certain occupants on higher floors to feel seasick. The technology of transporting water eighty floors up does not seem miraculous to a person becoming ill from seeing the water in a toilet bowl move back and forth with the motion of a tall building.

There are those who think that most modern skyscrapers are not really built for people. Donald Kuspit, a professor of art history and philosophy, thinks that the designers of nearly all of New York's high-rise

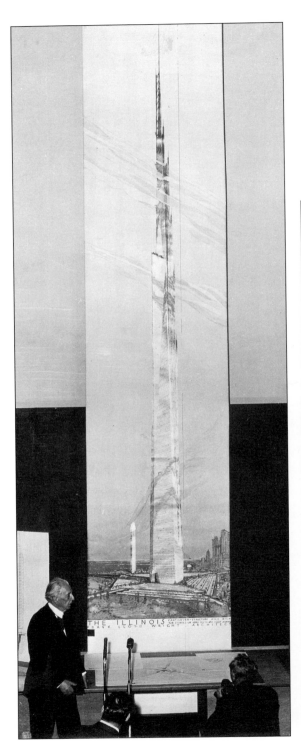

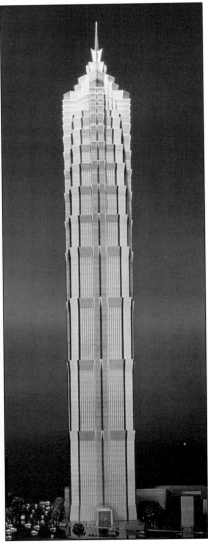

Left: Frank Lloyd Wright presents his mile-high concept.

Below: SOM's model of the Jin Mao Tower in Shanghai, a superskyscraper

architecture were "indifferent to the needs and feelings of the human beings who use it. . . . They built," he says, "to show their mastery of space and materials." Other people may respect the work of architects but are appalled at the dehumanizing messes developers can make. Donald Trump, for example, has built or renovated a number of valuable properties in midtown Manhattan in a gaudy and self-promoting manner. One of his earlier efforts is Trump Tower, a glittering, luxury apartment building on Fifth Avenue. Its first two floors are an indoor mall of chic boutiques decorated with huge amounts of gold-colored chrome and pink marble, dominated by a two-story waterfall. Another Fifth Avenue property, the General Motors Building, was acquired by Trump in 1998. In 1999 he had four-foot-high, gold-colored titanium wraparound letters attached to five of the building's white marble-clad support columns to spell out a golden shout, T-R-U-M-P.

The show-off activities of this flamboyant real estate mogul have earned him the hearty scorn of respected architecture critics and well-known architects. In a *New York Times* article on Trump, a former Dean of the Columbia School of Architecture is quoted as saying the developer is responsible for "an architecture so banal that it is an embarrassment."

Because they are forever debatable, issues of taste are almost impossible to control with municipal regulations. Issues of safety, however, can be controlled by city building codes. Of course, even with computer models and other kinds of pretesting, the building of skyscrapers can be a trial-and-error technology. Miscalculations will be made, but to avoid repeating them, revised building codes can reflect the lessons of each error. Other precautions are suggested by common sense even before a disaster happens. For example, Los Angeles has a regulation that any building above a certain height must have a landing pad on top so that helicopters can evacuate people during an earthquake or a fire. Consequently, I. M. Pei partner Henry N. Cobb included a helicopter landing pad in his design of the First Interstate Bank World Center in Los Angeles.

Steel workers hoist a flag for the "topping out" ceremony to celebrate the completion of the Empire State's frame at the eighty-sixth floor.

Skyscrapers are here to stay. They are part of our culture, and there are a lot of them. In fact, there are so many of them that most of the high-rise buildings seen on the world's urban skylines are anonymous. There are ugly buildings, boring skyscrapers, and magnificent towers. Many of them exist to make money, others are intended to impress people, and a few actually inspire awe. The one thing they all have in common is hard teamwork. The significance of this immensely complex collaborative effort in the building of skyscrapers is summed up in some construction notes for the Empire State Building. The writer was an employee of the building company, Starrett Bros. and Eken, Inc. "This massive building now stands as a majestic symbol of the enterprise and efficiency of our age—offering mute tribute to promoter, financier, architect, engineer, builder, artisan, and everyone who toiled to make it a reality—down to the humblest laborer."

*Looking straight up the stairwell of the Rookery in Chicago
can be a dizzying experience.*

NOTES

Citations not attributed to a source within the text follow.
References are to books cited in the bibliography.

CHAPTER ONE: INNOVATIONS

p. 9: "There is no economic need . . ." Quoted in Dupré, p. 7.

CHAPTER TWO: GOING UP

p. 18: "personally responsible for renting . . ." Quoted in Landau and
    Condit, p. 66.
p. 22: "the entire twenty-three-foot-high . . . " Landau, p. 31.

CHAPTER THREE: THE PHOENIX

p. 28: "I never felt so grateful in my life . . ." Quoted in Angle, p. 31.
p. 30: "excelled in both athletics and artistic projects . . ." Hines, p. 9.
p. 33: "the less plumbing, the less trouble . . . " Quoted in Hines, p. 52.

CHAPTER FOUR: MRS. JENNEY'S BIRDCAGE

p. 49: "This is the greatest meeting of artists . . ." Quoted in Hines, p. 90.

CHAPTER FIVE: NEW YORK SHOWS OFF

p. 57: "beyond a doubt his ego . . ." Landau and Condit, p. 382.

CHAPTER SIX: OUTSIDE INSIDE

p. 76: "Mies believed . . ." Dupré, p. 51.

CHAPTER SEVEN: ALL OVER THE WORLD

p. 101: "This massive building . . ." Quoted in Willis, ed., *Building the Empire State*, p.77.

BIBLIOGRAPHY

ALBION, ROBERT GREENHALGH. *The Rise of New York Port, 1815–1860.* New York: Charles Scribner's Sons, 1939 (copyright renewed 1967).

ANGLE, PAUL M. ed. *The Great Chicago Fire Described in Seven Letters.* Chicago: Chicago Historical Society, 1946.

BENNETT, DAVID. *Skyscrapers: Form and Function.* New York: Simon & Schuster, 1995.

CANNELL, MICHAEL T. *I. M. Pei: Mandarin of Modernism.* New York: Carol Southern Books (Potter/Crown/Random House), 1995.

CERVER, FRANCISCO ASENIO. *The Architecture of Skyscrapers.* New York: Arco for Hearst Books International, 1997.

DOHERTY, CRAIG A. and KATHERINE M. DOHERTY. *The Sears Tower.* Woodbridge, CT: Blackbirch Press, 1995.

DUPRÉ, JUDITH. *Skyscrapers.* New York: Black Dog & Leventhal Publishers, 1996.

GIBLIN, JAMES CROSS. *The Skyscraper Book*. New York: Thomas Y. Crowell, 1981.

GOLDBERGER, PAUL. *On the Rise: Architecture and Design in a Postmodern Age*. New York: Times Books, 1983.

HINES, THOMAS S. *Burnham of Chicago: Architect and Planner*. Chicago: University of Chicago Press, 1979.

HUXTABLE, ADA LOUISE. *Goodbye History, Hello Hamburger: An Anthology of Architectural Delights and Disasters*. Washington, D. C.: Preservation Press, 1986.

_____. *The Tall Building Artistically Reconsidered*. Berkeley, CA: University of California Press, 1984 & 1992.

LANDAU, SARAH BRADFORD. *George B. Post, Architect: Picturesque Designer and Determined Realist*. New York: The Montacelli Press, 1998.

_____ and CARL W. CONDIT. *Rise of the New York Skyscraper 1865–1913*. New Haven, CT: Yale University Press, 1996.

MILLER, DONALD L. *City of the Century: The Epic of Chicago and the Making of America*. New York: Touchstone, Simon & Schuster, 1996.

MUMFORD, LEWIS. *Sticks and Stones: A Study of American Architecture and Civilization*. New York: Dover, 1955.

NASH, ERIC. *New York's 50 Best Skyscrapers*. New York: City & Company, 1997.

PELLI, CESAR. *Cesar Pelli Buildings and Projects 1965–1990*. New York: Rizzoli, 1990.

PETROSKI, HENRY. *Remaking the World: Adventures in Engineering*. New York: Alfred A. Knopf, 1997.

RAMSEY, CHARLES G. and HAROLD R. SLEEPER. *Architectural Graphic Standards*. New York: John Wiley & Sons, Inc., 1970.

RICCIUTI, EDWARD. *America's Top 10 Skyscrapers*. Woodbridge, CT: Blackbirch Press, 1998.

SCHULZE, FRANZ and KEVIN HARRINGTON, eds. *Chicago's Famous Buildings*. Chicago: University of Chicago Press, 1993.

SCULLY, VINCENT. *American Architecture and Urbanism.* New York: Henry Holt & Company, 1988.

TWOMBLY, ROBERT. *Louis Sullivan: His Life and Work.* New York: Viking, 1986.

VAN LEEUWEN, THOMAS, A. P. *The Skyward Trend of Thought: The Metaphysics of the American Skyscraper.* Cambridge, MA: The MIT Press, 1986.

WILLIS, CAROL, ed. *Building the Empire State.* New York: W. W. Norton & Company, 1998.

WILLIS, CAROL. *Form Follows Finance: Skyscrapers and Skylines in New York and Chicago.* New York: Princeton Architectural Press, 1995.

WISEMAN, CARTER. *I. M. Pei: A Profile in American Architecture.* New York: Harry N. Abrams, Inc., 1990.

_____. *Shaping a Nation: Twentieth Century American Architecture and Its Makers.* New York: W. W. Norton & Company, 1998.

WOLFE, GERARD R. *Chicago: In and Around the Loop.* New York: McGraw-Hill, 1996.

WOLFE, TOM. *From Bauhaus to Our House.* New York: Farrar Straus & Giroux, 1981.

ZIGA, CHARLES J. *New York Landmarks: A Collection of Architecture and Historical Details.* New York: Dovetail Books, 1993.

PICTURE CREDITS

INDEX